ANKYLOSAURUS
(an-KIE-loh-sore-us)

TYRANNOSAURUS REX
(tie-RAN-oh-sore-us rex)

APATOSAURUS
(ah-PAT-oh-sore-us)

To Michael and Edward, with love
T.K.

For Lucy and Harry
S.W.

First published in 2013 by Scholastic Children's Books
This edition first published in 2014
Euston House, 24 Eversholt Street
London NW1 1DB
a division of Scholastic Ltd
www.scholastic.co.uk
London ~ New York ~ Toronto ~ Sydney ~ Auckland
Mexico City ~ New Delhi ~ Hong Kong

ISBN 978-1-4351-5651-7

Lot #:
2 4 6 8 10 9 7 5 3 1
07/14

Dinosaurs
in the Supermarket

By Timothy Knapman

Illustrated by Sarah Warburton

There are **dinosaurs** in the **supermarket!**
Look, they're everywhere!
If only grown-ups noticed them
They'd get a frightful scare.

There's T. rex gobbling sausages...

Stegosaurus spilling beans...

Apatosaurs chucking frozen peas
Are filling the aisles with greens!

There are **dinosaurs** in the supermarket!
But when I tell my mom
They hide until she looks away...

And then...right back they come!

Ankylosaurus and his cart
Crash into all those cans.
The pterosaurs go flying
And end up in the flans!

Triceratops squirt chocolate sauce.
Hadrosaurs scoff cake.
Iguanodons chuck toilet rolls.
What a MONSTER MESS they make!

"Our supermarket's ruined!"
The check-out staff despair.
"In the parking lot there's ice cream,
We have ketchup everywhere!"

"There are DINOSAURS in the supermarket!"
I shout out straight away.
"Look, their custard footprints
Must be clear as day!"

"DINOSAURS in the SUPERMARKET?
Please don't put us on!"

I point to where I saw them...

...But the dinosaurs have gone.

If this goes on much longer,
They'll think that I'm to blame.
So I find those sneaky dinosaurs
And say, "Let's play a game...

...called Supermarket Cleanup."
I give each one a mop.
They plunge them in the suds and – SPLAT!
They splash and swoosh and slop!

In no time, things are shining bright.
The grown-ups say, "Well done!
This boy here cleaned the supermarket."
My mom says, "That's my son!"

But I DIDN'T. It was DINOSAURS!
They don't believe it's true...

...Till hordes of soapy dinosaurs
Jump out, shouting... **"BOO!"**

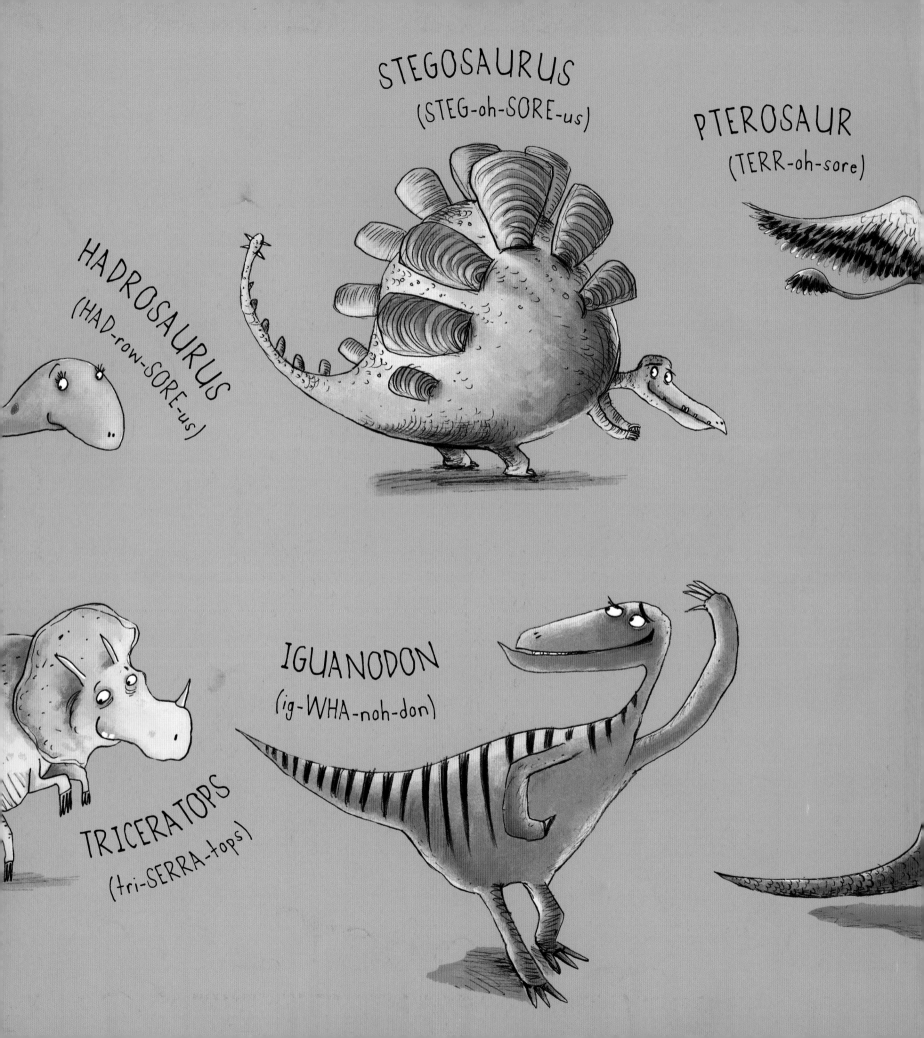

STEGOSAURUS
(STEG-oh-SORE-us)

PTEROSAUR
(TERR-oh-sore)

HADROSAURUS
(HAD-row-SORE-us)

TRICERATOPS
(tri-SERRA-tops)

IGUANODON
(ig-WHA-noh-don)